Alice

Book 1 in the Princess Alice series of online
safety adventures

www.southcrater.com

Look out for

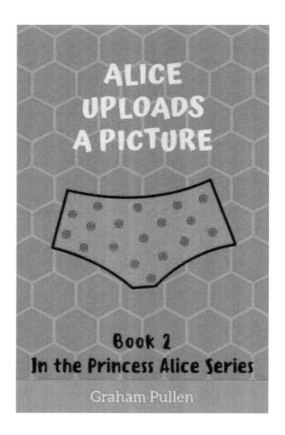

ALICE
UPLOADS
A PICTURE

Book 2
In the Princess Alice Series

Graham Pullen

Alice & The Troll

Book 1 in the Princess Alice series of online safety adventures

By Graham Pullen

Published by South Crater Ltd

Brighton UK

First Printing, 2019

ISBN 978-1-9160559-0-2

Published by
South Crater Ltd
www.southcrater.com

Additional Images (moon & snail)
copyright Hollie-April Pullen

For Hollie-April

my perfect pickle

Contents

Prologue

Princess Alice is a werewolf but not as scary as you might think. She has turquoise eyes, a purple nose and fur the brightest pink.

Rumour says werewolves don't like people, but that simply isn't true. They laugh and play and love their moms and dads, like me and you.

So here we have a story about having fun online. I hope that you enjoy it and you learn at the same time.

Being online is a source of fun as long as you put safety first. Then remember how to spot a troll as they really are the worst.

Chapter 1

A Bored Princess

'I think' sighed Princess Alice 'that the world is flat. The moon is made of cheese and the bogey man is real'.

'Yes, Your Highness' snapped the royal guards, standing to attention. Their polished tunic buttons glistened in the morning sun.

3

It was the weekend and the young princess was bored. Being a princess could be a really boring job.

Other than her parents, and her school teachers of course, no one would ever disagree with anything that she said. Even when what she said was very, very silly.

Why is it, Alice wondered, when you are a princess, everyone is so polite to you all of the time. Everyone calls you 'your highness' or 'your royal highness' no matter what you call them in return. Princess Alice liked to make up silly names for the guards.

She wondered what it would be like to have an argument.

Not a big noisy shouting match. Just to argue and debate a different point of view. She longed for someone to say 'No You are wrong!', instead of 'Yes your highness'.

Now more than ever, Princess Alice longed for a new friend. A friend that didn't know she was a royal.

The princess sat staring at the rose Garden. She watched a black and yellow striped bumble-bee gently floating between the flowers.

She thought how easy it must be to be a bee. To just fly to the next garden if the one you were in no longer had nectar for you. It was then that she had a great idea.

'I must find a new friend, in a different garden' she muttered to herself.

What she meant was that she needed to find a friend far away in a different kingdom. A friend who didn't know she was a princess.

It couldn't be anyone too local as she was so well known.

Growing up, Alice noticed that everyone recognised her. Maybe it was because of her mum's picture on the postage stamps and her dads face on all of the bank notes. Being constantly told that 'you look just like them' was definitely not a compliment she liked.

She had never had to find a friend before. The castle was always so busy with royal balls, parties and visitors coming and going. Friends usually found her.

At school the other girls and boys had many friends. They were always talking to each other on their mobile phones.

They sent text messages and pictures even, Princess Alice recalled with a chuckle, when they were sat next to each other.

As she sat sniggering to herself, the kitchen maid came out to pick fresh herbs from the garden.

'Good morning' shouted the princess.

'Good Morning your-highness' came the familiar reply.

'May I ask?' continued the princess 'do you have many friends?'

The maid stopped plucking at the fresh mint growing in the garden. She straightened herself to stand.

Thinking for a moment, the maid said

'Yes, I suppose that I do your-highness. That is, I have enough friends not to be lonely. I have not too many as to have time to meet up with them all every now and then'.

The princess's smile grew bigger at the thoughtful reply coming from the maid.

To be honest, the princess could not remember the maid's name.

Not because she was a maid — the princess spoke to everyone in the castle and thought no more or less of them whatever their job — but because she met so many people, she sometimes forgot who was who.

This, she thought, was someone who must be able to help her find a friend.

'and if you needed to make a new friend? Say for an empty seat at the cinema or to make up the numbers for a netball team?' the princess wondered out loud.

Thinking for a moment the maid replied 'well I should go online and look on social media. Friends of friends or maybe people in groups who like the things I like. That is where I would start'

The princess thanked the maid politely. She apologised for not remembering her name and headed off feeling very excited.

The princess was smiling a huge grin that went from ear to ear.

Of course, she had heard of social media Alice lived in a castle, not on the moon .....

…. although on particularly boring wet weekends she liked to pretend the castle was on the moon.

She made the guards wear fish bowls on their heads – minus the fish of course – and walk in giant steps as if on the face of the moon.

The guards seemed to enjoy it too, talking to each other in crackly voices and talking about 'giant steps'.

Social media, Alice recalled, is made up of lots of different websites and applications where friends shared picture of their pets, pictures of their legs sat by a pool on holiday (that Alice always thought looked a lot like sausages) or pictures of their dinner.

Websites where friends kept in touch with other friends that had moved away.

Even friends in different kingdoms

Chapter 2

Parental Control

So Princess Alice had a plan. She would go online, create a profile and find a friend. She had spent a lot of time thinking about the type of friend she wanted.

There were so many choices

- a boy or a girl

- her age, older or younger

- werewolf or not werewolf

- royal or not royal

She had scribbled a list, changed her mind, changed it back and then changed it again many times over. Finally, she was certain that she knew exactly the friend she was looking for.

Now step one was to choose a website and go online to set up her account.

As the princess typed the website address into her computer, a most unusual thing happened. The screen froze and a warning popped up in big red letters.

This Page has been blocked

by Parental Controls

'Urrrrrgh!' exclaimed the princess.

She remembered now the talk with her father, King Aldric. Recalling the day the castle was visited by a geeky looking computer whizz.

The king had explained how he had installed special software to stop her visiting websites that had scary pictures or nasty comments left by internet trolls.

Trolls, the king had told her, liked nothing more than to go online and leave nasty comments for no reason. Princess Alice wondered why they would do that.

Then she remembered she had once met a troll on the edge of the woods that border the werewolf kingdom.

He was dragging a large wooden club along the ground behind him leaving a trail of upturned flowers.

18

The princess didn't usually judge people but she thought the troll looked the sort of person that would get joy from making others upset.

As she sat staring at the screen wondering what to do next, Alice's mother Queen Adela came into the room smiling.

'Good morning my dear, what are you doing on the computer?' asked the queen.

'Nothing mum'.

The princess quickly closed-down the computer. She sat looking at a beetle walking across the castle floor. She picked it up and placed it, gently, on the tree branch just outside of the open window.

Queen Adela was very wise and made-up real-world rules for using the computer.

A neatly hand-written sticky note was stuck on the side of the computer. Over time the note had been torn and faded. Now only the first two rules remained

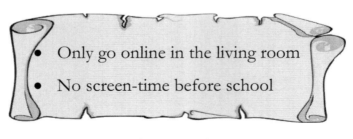

- Only go online in the living room
- No screen-time before school

Princess Alice thought long and hard. Her father was always very busy and whilst he always tried his best, he often forgot to finish what he started. Queen Adela was always asking him to finish one job before starting the next.

'That's it!' she exclaimed 'my tablet'.

'What's what dear?'

'Nothing mum'

The princess remembered that the computer whizz had installed software on the family computer. He had installed it on her smart phone too, but not on her tablet.

She knew she would have to be mischievous. Smiling to herself, she tucked her tablet device between her school books.

Later that evening Princess Alice kissed her mother goodnight, picked up the bundle of books and her tablet and strode off towards her bedroom.

'Don't you want to stay up and watch television a little longer' shouted King Aldric.

'No thank you daddy' she replied skipping off down the corridor with the tablet clenched tight.

Once in her room, the princess closed the door and sat on her bed looking at her tablet. She knew that she was breaking the rules set by her mother by going online in her room on her own.

She stopped for a moment and began to worry. What if she found pictures so scary that she would not sleep, or worse still, sleep but dream horrible nightmares?

Her heart pounding, the princess turned on the tablet. The screen lit up as the device played a little tune to say that it was ready to use.

The princess stopped breathing just for a second, listening at the door to her room. Had anyone heard the tune play?

After what seemed like ages (about 2 minutes) she was convinced that no one was coming.

The princess picked up the small, oblong device and running her fingers across the screen opened a window to the social media website the maid had told her about.

The screen stared back – in big bold letters the instructions read:

and the princess gently tapped the screen.

Chapter 3

The Profile

The screen burst into life with box after box to complete. First name. Last name. Where do you live. The princess completed each one with glee.

Now to choose a username. Nothing too princess-y or to regal sounding. Alice pondered and slowly typed

K – A – T – R – I- N – A- 1- 2- 3

Looking back at the screen Alice smiled and pressed **GO**. Now she had a new online identity. She looked in the mirror. 'Hello – I am Katrina, pleased to meet you'.

Then the tablet beeped loudly and displayed a new message.

<Click to confirm you are over 13 years old >

But the princess was not over 13. She was very much under 13. Her palms were a little sweaty and she felt a little sick in her tummy. As she pondered what to do next, she reached to brush a bug from the side of her tablet.

The castle was old and made of stone with cracks and gaps here and there. Alice was often visited by all kinds of insects from the local woods.

She didn't mind as she loved bugs. The princess would often keep them in a jar beside her bed. Only for a day or two as a pet before releasing them back into the woods.

As she picked up a very small shield bug, her thumb brushed the screen. The tablet played a fanfare and showed a new message

<Set up complete – hello Katrina123 >

Oh well, she thought, what was done was done. Next, she went about joining groups where like-minded people might be. Joining groups like

- ❖ **I Love Horses**
- ❖ **Painting for beginners**
- ❖ **Flowers & gardens**
- ❖ **Pets**

When she was finished, closing down the tablet and tucking it back in her pile of books, Alice suddenly felt a little guilty.

Princess Alice had broken the rules. She had gone online on her own, in her bedroom and to a site her father had blocked.

Oh well, she shrugged her shoulders, nothing bad had happened. They hadn't even noticed when she told a small white lie about her age.

The princess yawned, pulled the covers up over her shoulders and fell asleep.

'Morning my dear – time to get up, you don't want to be late for school. Don't forget your books, shall I help with these?' her father's voice boomed the usual 7am alarm call.

'Oh no daddy, I will carry them' Alice replied. She tucked them under her arm and headed off to start the daily routine - cleaning teeth, eating breakfast and dressing ready for the school bus.

As the rest of the castle busied itself, preparing for another visiting dignitary, the princess turned on her tablet. Logging on she could not believe her eyes. Message after message filled the screen.

What surprised her was not the number of messages, she was a princess after all. The surprise was that they all said the same thing.

Please send pics

What should she do now?

Chapter 4

Blue

The princess didn't know what to do. She turned off the tablet and headed out of the castle gates. Climbing onto the school bus, Alice was deep in thought.

At break time, Alice sat quietly in the playground still thinking. She couldn't go to her parents for advice. She would have to admit breaking the rules.

'That's it' she thought 'I will ask my friends instead, they will know what to do'.

Alice's best friend at school was Agnes. Agnes was a few months older so had her birthday first every year. In Alice's eyes that made her a lot more grown up. Agnes also had a mobile phone already and was always online.

Agnes' started Alice 'I need some advice please'.

'The princess went on to explain the problem to her BFF.

Agnes listened intently. When the princess had finished, Agnes smiled. Her response was short and to the point, as she always was.

'Alice, your life hasn't gone out of kilter, just do what we all do and use a filter'.

That was it, why hadn't the princess thought of it already. Giggling loudly, Alice posed as Agnes clicked away on her phone.

When the two girls were happy with the shot, they started to play with picture filters. Adding and then removing flowers, glasses, birds and funny ears.

'No' said Alice, 'I don't want Katrina to look silly. I just want her to look, well, less like me'.

Agnes thought for a moment and then clicked through several screens too quickly for Alice to follow.

'How is that?' asked Agnes.

Alice looked at the picture of Katrina filling the screen. Her bright blue eyes had turned dark brown. Her purple nose was black. But most striking of all, her beautiful pink fur was now the most electric blue.

'Perfect!' she exclaimed and taking the phone logged on again and uploaded the picture to her profile. 'Hello Katrina' you are a beautiful blue werewolf'.

Chapter 5

Troll

Troll sat in his cave, staring at the empty cage on the top shelf.

Troll didn't have a name. In troll society names were not needed. Instead trolls referred to each other simply as 'her' or 'him' or 'that one'. It was a very confusing system.

If you ever listened to a troll conversation it might go something like this.

Troll 1: 'I saw him with new club'

Troll 2: 'What him?'

Troll 1: 'Him what lives in cave by river'

Troll 2: 'Him what lives with her with curly
        hair?'

Troll 1: 'No him what lives with her with nice
        hat'

Trolls also spoke differently to you or me. They missed out words or said them in the wrong order. It really wasn't a problem for the trolls as they were not very social anyway.

Although they were not social creatures, Troll really wanted to have a pet. He didn't know what sort of a pet, just one that would fit inside his cage.

Now you might think that would limit his choices. The other thing to know about trolls is that they are very, very big. The average troll grows 3 to 4 meters tall. As they are so big, their caves are big, and their possessions are big too.

Every troll's favourite possession is their club. Every troll owns one and will always carry it with them outside of the cave.

Carried over the shoulder or dragged along the ground, the club is never left behind.

Groups of trolls can often be found comparing clubs and club jealously leads to many troll fights.

Trolls use their club for many different jobs. To clear a path through the forest. To break down branches used for firewood. But the most important job of the club is to brush away bugs.

Trolls hate bugs. If truth were known, trolls are scared of all bugs. Not just the ones that scurry along quickly like spiders or ants.

Trolls are just as scared of slower insects like snails and worms.

Anyway, Troll's cage was actually so big that the average human child, or werewolf, would fit nicely inside.

Troll also had lots of electronic things. He had 5 televisions, 4 digital radios, 3 computers, 2 laptops and a smartphone.

Another little-known fact about trolls is that they are actually quite rich. They don't have jobs or go to work and they do not steal, well not really.

Trolls discovered long ago that humans like to throw coins in water.

It started way back when. People liked to throw money into wells and make a wish but they never thought about what happened to all of the coins.

Now some wells are for charity and will have a sign saying something like 'all donations for save the whales' or 'for friends of the aardvarks'.

Trolls realised that no one reads the signs, so set up their own network of wells.

At first the trolls would leave a handwritten sign saying - 'money in here is all for trolls' or 'trolls' friends please'. After a while they stopped leaving signs.

If you ever throw money into a well or fountain with no sign, chances are you are giving your money to trolls.

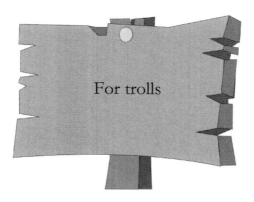

For trolls

Troll sighed. A sigh so strong it blew closed the open fridge door. He turned on the computer and, poking at the over-sized keyboard with his big sausage-like fingers, typed one word into his favourite search-engine.

P-E-T

The screen showed rows upon rows of pet related websites.

>> Best pet shops for trolls on a budget
>>Caring for your pet
>> Pet poop scoopers – half price today
>> Pet group –for all things pet related

Troll scrolled down the list.

'don't wanna buy nothing'

'don't got a pet to care for'

'don't wanna pooper scooper'

Then he stopped and hovered over the link

>>Pet group ....

he clicked and waited for the page to load.

As the page opened up, pictures loaded one by
one filling the screen with colour.

A pet python. A very fat cat. A sausage-dog. Stick insects, fish and all manner of other creatures.

Troll's eyes were drawn to something else on the page. Under the heading – **New Members** – was a picture of a werewolf with the most beautiful blue fur that troll had ever seen.

Troll rocked back in his chair, the front two feet left the floor and as troll fell backwards propelling his head towards the floor, he said out loud

'Troll found his pet'.

Chapter 6

The Trap

Troll was so excited. He took the cage down from the top shelf. He put his hand inside and wiped away the cobwebs and the used chewing gum deposited there weeks earlier.

'Lots of room for werewolf' he said to himself.

Troll placed it back neatly on the shelf, after checking the key still worked and the door to the cage could be kept locked shut.

Troll had thought lots about the bright blue werewolf he had found online. He decided he was going to keep her as a pet and would rename her Fluffy. (Katrina, he decided, sounded far too odd for a pet).

He also hatched a plan to lure the werewolf into the woods and catch it in a trap. It was an especially good plan as usually trolls are not very clever at all.

Troll left the cave carrying his club, as usual, and a shovel. When he came to a clearing on the edge of the woods, he dug a small pit.

Small that is by troll standards, plenty big enough for a werewolf to fall into and not be able to climb out.

When the pit was dug, he used his club to drag a criss-cross of sticks and leaves across the top to make the perfect trap.

Walking back to his cave, troll thought about how he would lure the werewolf into the woods.

It was then he remembered that, unlike trolls who liked nothing more than to spend all day sitting around with their club, werewolves loved adventure.

The troll settled down in his favourite computer chair. He turned on the computer and clicked the link

>>Pet Group

Katrina was online. (The screen told troll that by highlighting her name in green). Troll started to type. As he typed, Alice sat alone in her room on her tablet.

Alice had been very excited by her first exchange of messages. Maybe this was the friend that she had been looking for?

She checked the screen. The message had come from a user called Rollt. That's an unusual name she thought, he must come from a very faraway place. Rollt didn't have a picture, just a black silhouette.

As Alice (Katrina123) and Troll (Rollt) typed, the conversation went like this:

Rollt: Hello. Your fur, I like

Katrina123: Thank you. Do you like pets

Rollt: Pets. I am getting new pet soon

Rollt: Cage is ready

Katrina123: You must be very excited

Rollt: Yes very excited. Pet come soon

Rollt: You like see my pet?

Katrina123: Yes I would, very much

Katrina 123: Could you send a picture?

Alice was so excited. She had already met a new friend and he was going to have a new pet and would send her pictures.

He had a funny name and mixed his words around a little so he sounded very exotic.

The princess was sure that they would become good friends. New messages filled her inbox –

Rollt: Will you meet in woods?
Rollt: Show pet I can!
Rollt: No tell parents, or in trouble we get

Alice felt a little disappointed. He wasn't that far off at all. Still, he hadn't called her 'Your Highness' and didn't know who she really was.

The screen lit up and her tablet beeped once more as a new message appeared.

Rollt: An ADVENTURE it will be
Rollt: I means it be an ADVENTURE.
Rollt: Visiting I am for ADVENTURE

The princess thought for a while. The cursor on her screen flashed patiently waiting for a response. 'At least' she thought 'he was only visiting and didn't live here so could still be from a far-away exotic land'.

Should she go?

What would her parents say?

How would she explain her change in colour if they did meet?

So many questions filled her head. Princess Alice thought so hard it made her head hurt. Above all it WOULD be an ADVENTURE and she loved adventures.

In that moment Princess Alice made her own plan. She would sneak out of the castle, telling no one where she was going. She would cover her fur in an old raincoat (the maids kept them by the door to the garden in case of rain).

She would meet her new friend, look at pictures of his new pet and have a great adventure that they would talk about online after he went back to his own kingdom.

Katrina123: Yes, I WILL MEET YOU

Troll grinned from ear to ear. Not a nice, happy grin but the kind of grin that a Cheshire cat makes when he has caught a mouse.

They kept on exchanging messages. Agreed a day and a time. Rollt (troll) explained where he would be waiting at the clearing on the edge of the wood.

As they both closed down their devices, the princess and the troll shared the exact same thought. The plan was set and they were going to have the most fantastic day on Saturday.

Chapter 7

The Meeting

The rest of the week was almost unbearable for the princess. She was bursting with secrets but couldn't tell anyone.

Rollt had insisted time and time again, as they arranged the details, that if she told anyone he would get into lots of trouble as his new pet was meant to be a secret birthday present

Oh yes – he also mentioned that it was his birthday on Saturday, another reason for the Princess to go and meet him as there would be birthday cake.

Alice just giggled and looked away when her friends asked what she was doing at the weekend. 'Nothing special' she replied, her shoes digging circles into the ground as she looked down to her feet.

The school days seemed to get longer and longer. Every day the princess sneaked her tablet into her room and exchanged more messages with Rollt.

She told him all about her family, leaving out the bit about them being the king and queen, and all about her friends at school. In return Rollt didn't say much about himself. Alice thought he must be shy so didn't ask him for his picture just in case he got upset.

When Saturday finally arrived, it was a grey, damp, drizzly rain day.

Alice knew when the weather was turning wetter or colder as more and more bugs would crawl through the cracks in the castle to visit her.

This morning she shared her room with a mix of lady bugs, beetles and woodlice. These were her pets she thought to herself chuckling.

As she ate her breakfast, her father King Aldric seemed to take great interest in her day.

'What my dear are you up to today? He boomed from behind his newspaper - the Werewolf Times.

'Nothing much' she replied 'I am going to play in the garden on the edge of the woods'. A half-lie she thought would be better than a complete lie.

'In the garden?' he half put down his paper and peered over the top 'in this weather?'

You're right daddy, I will play in the covered courtyard'

Alice had to make an excuse for not being inside the castle in case he came looking. 'I want to make a new bug-house to keep them covered up from the rain'.

The king looked puzzled. 'Bugs, pets, rain, I will never understand what goes on in your head'. He picked up the newspaper and continued reading the headlines –

New Wishing Well Appears on Village Green.

Troll was also eating breakfast.

He didn't live with his parents anymore. Trolls were expected to leave home as soon as they were old enough to build their own well and become self-sufficient.

As he finished breakfast troll wiped his hands on his shirt, already stained with orange juice, butter and what was possibly tomato ketchup.

He picked up his club and left the cave strolling confidently into the woods humming away (very out of tune).

Princess Alice had also finished breakfast. She wiped her hands on a napkin which she folded neatly and placed into the washing basket in the kitchen. 'Thank you Your Highness' said the kitchen maid, making Alice jump.

'Would you fetch more toast for my father' asked the princess. The maid smiled politely and hurried off to find more bread. Alice slipped on an old raincoat and let herself out of the door into the garden.

As the maid brought more toast, the king looked at her in surprise. The Queen normally stopped him having seconds.

In the corner of his eye the king noticed a maid, dressed in an old raincoat, climbing over the garden wall and heading off towards the woods.

'What a strange day' he thought to himself. Then he sat back, picked up another piece of toast and started smearing butter on both sides. Licking his lips, the king forgot all about seeing a maid clambering over the garden wall.

As Troll marched through the woods, he swung his club up high making big circles and singing a song in his booming, disjointed voice

'Her fur is blue, her eyes are dark, she thinks Troll wants to meet her. To be her friend but I want a pet and so I'm going to keep her.

Held in a cage, she will adorn the top shelf way up high. Until one day I'm bored of her and bake her in a pie'

Chapter 8

Taking Leaves

Climbing the garden wall had been very hard for the princess. In school PE lessons she had to climb a rope and ring the bell at the top but never quite made it. Climbing, she decided, was definitely not her thing.

She stopped to catch her breath. Resting on an old tree stump, the princess still thought that she was going to a secret rendezvous with a new friend.

Had the princess known that Rollt was in fact Troll she would have run home as fast as her legs would carry her. Instead she rested and looked again at the map that Rollt had sent, the clearing wasn't far away now.

As she rested, the wind began to blow. The wind whipped up leaves and small twigs that caught in the over-sized coat. Still, at least the rain had stopped

Alice took off the coat and, folding it into a small bundle, stooped to place it in a hollow tree trunk. for safekeeping.

At that moment troll came thundering past, still booming out his dreadful song.

'Held in a cage, she will adorn the top shelf way up high. Until one day I'm bored of her and bake her in a pie'

As Alice heard the words it took some time for her to realize the danger she was in. What should she do?

The princess thought of running for home. The troll was so close that any noise or sudden movement would surely attract his attention

For the first time in her life Princess Alice felt very scared. Very scared and very alone. How she wished now that she had told someone where she was going. Her friends, her parents or one of the castle guards.

If only one of the guards had seen her leave, wondered why a maid was climbing the wall and had followed her ready to rescue her now and carry her home.

Alice waited. No guard came. No one called her name or offered her help as they always did in the castle. In fact, it had gone very quiet indeed.

The troll had stopped singing and his footsteps could no longer be heard snapping twigs and clearing bushes as he charged through the under-growth.

He must have reached the clearing.

As Alice wondered what would become of her, she had the most brilliant idea. Such a great idea that it might just save her from a horrible fate at the hands of a troll.

The more the idea formed in her head, the more she knew it would work. Rollt, that is Troll, wasn't looking for her. He was looking for a blue werewolf called Katrina.

Most of all she knew her plan would work as it is a well-known fact that

all trolls are twits.

But still she had to be careful, she was a princess and her parents had plenty of money. If a troll wanted one thing more than a pet, it was money (and no one ever worked out where they got so much money from).

The princess knelt and began to pick up handfuls of mud and leaves which she used to cover her fur. As she smeared her fur with dirt, she felt a lot less princess-like.

The rain had also brought out her friends the slugs.

Alice rounded them up and, offering them a lift, popped them onto her shoulders. No respectful troll would want slugs in his cave.

However dirty they are themselves it is a well-known fact that Trolls hate slugs.

They try all-sorts of ways to keep them out of their caves. Sprinkling salt, broken egg shells and even strips of copper metal to stop them coming in the door.

If you ever see this sort of behaviour from a human, they are probably descended from trolls.

Taking a deep breath, Princess Alice began shouting.

'No, I haven't seen your new friend and I won't go to the park. You are the rudest werewolf I have ever met with blue fur and eyes so dark.'

Troll heard the commotion. As he turned and caught sight of Alice, his voice boomed.

'Blue one. Which way he did go?'

Princess Alice stayed silent. She lifted her arm and pointed into the forest.

The troll looked at the princess and, as he turned and started off into the woods, he could be heard muttering.

'Yuk slugs, Troll hates slugs. Slugs bad'.

The princess waited until the Troll was out of sight before running back to the castle as fast as she could go.

Chapter 9

Confession Time

King Aldric and Queen Adela were playing ping-pong in the games room when they heard the commotion.

'Double the guard. Search the castle grounds for trolls!' The Sergeant-at-arms barked orders to the castle guards.

'Come on now dearies, let's get you back out in the wet'. The head gardener was carefully plucking slugs from Alice's fur and placing them side by side on a large cabbage leaf.

'Run the bath, extra bubbles' shrieked the Princess's lady-in-waiting.

'Oh my!' Queen Adela exclaimed.

'What on earth?' asked King Aldric.

Princess Alice, bundled in a blanket and carried into the castle by the biggest, strongest guard on duty, stood shaking and dripping wet mud.

'Mummy, daddy, she began. 'I am so sorry. I have been so silly'.

It seemed as if everyone in the castle had been there to help Alice from the moment she ran back into the castle garden.

In no time she was clean again, her pink fur no longer matted with mud. She sat in front of the fire drinking a huge mug of hot chocolate.

(With a double helping of whizzy cream and marshmallows. Cook thought it best to help with the shock of so much excitement).

Between sips, Alice told her mother and father all about what had happened. How she had broken the rules. The fake profile pictures. The secret meeting. The excitement at making a new friend.

When she told them about the troll, King Aldric looked super cross and Queen Adela super scared.

They all agreed that Alice had a lucky escape. Alice promised not to break the rules again and Queen Adela promised to help her find a pen-friend safely, together next time.

Troll meanwhile had spent the remainder of the day wandering the forest. He never found his blue furry pet. Eventually as the sun began to set, Troll headed back to his cave looking glum.

As he slumped back into his chair and looked at his empty cage, Troll started to hatch a new plan to find a pet. At that moment this computer beeped, a new member had joined Pets group. Troll began to type

'Hello. I am Rollt'.

Epilogue

So, this ends our story, at times it has been scary. I hope now, like Princess Alice, when online you will be wary.

Play your games and have your fun, but if you chat be wise. Remember that behind the screen may be a troll in disguise

The End

Stay Safe Online

&

Remember to Have Fun

Coming Soon

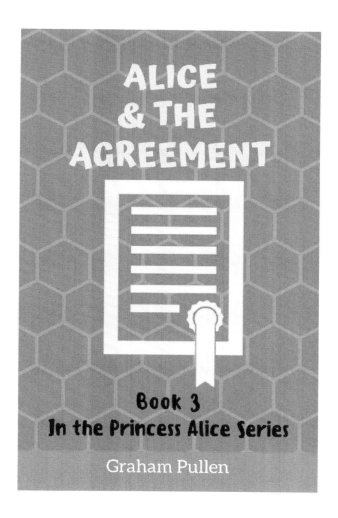

Printed in Great Britain
by Amazon

76859046R00061